Stone Girl
Bone Girl

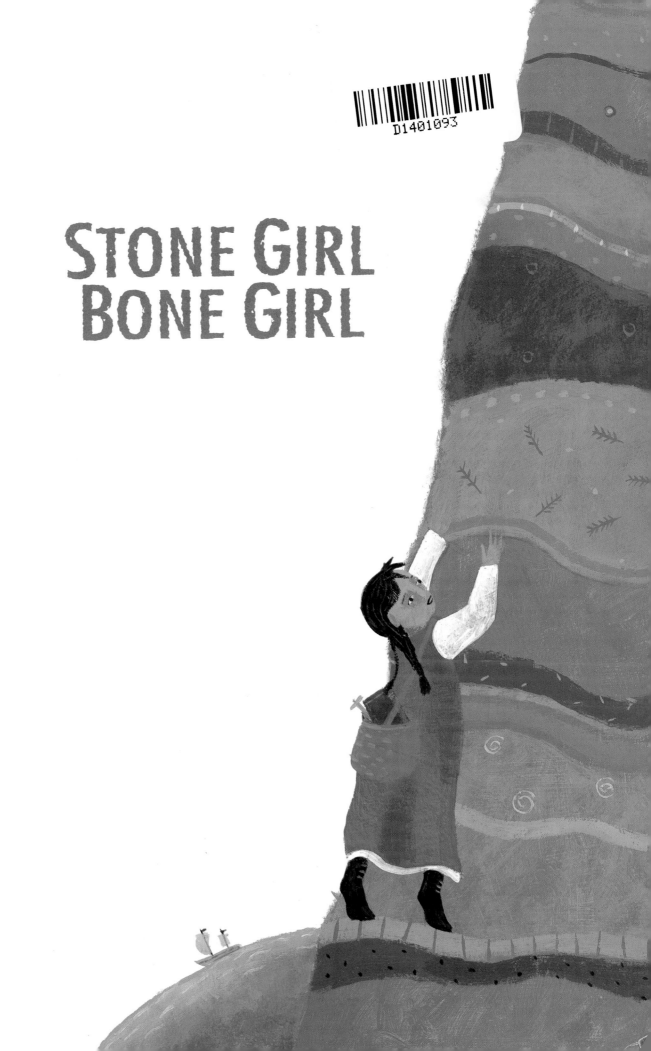

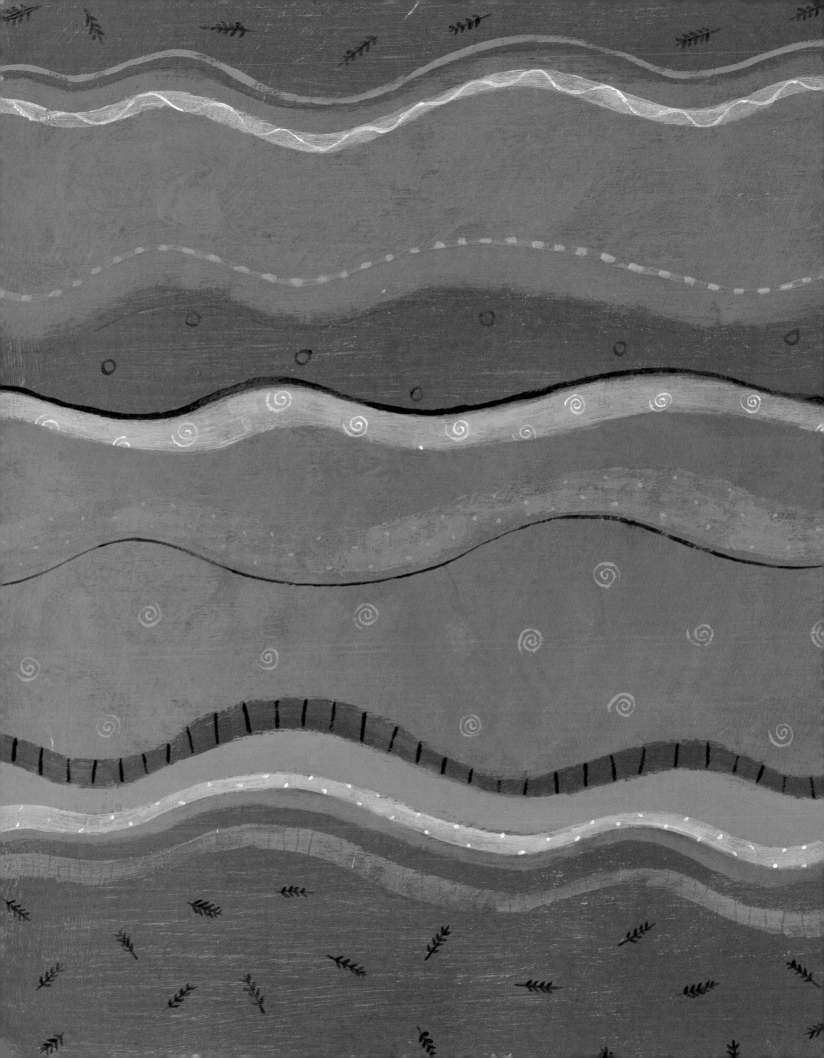

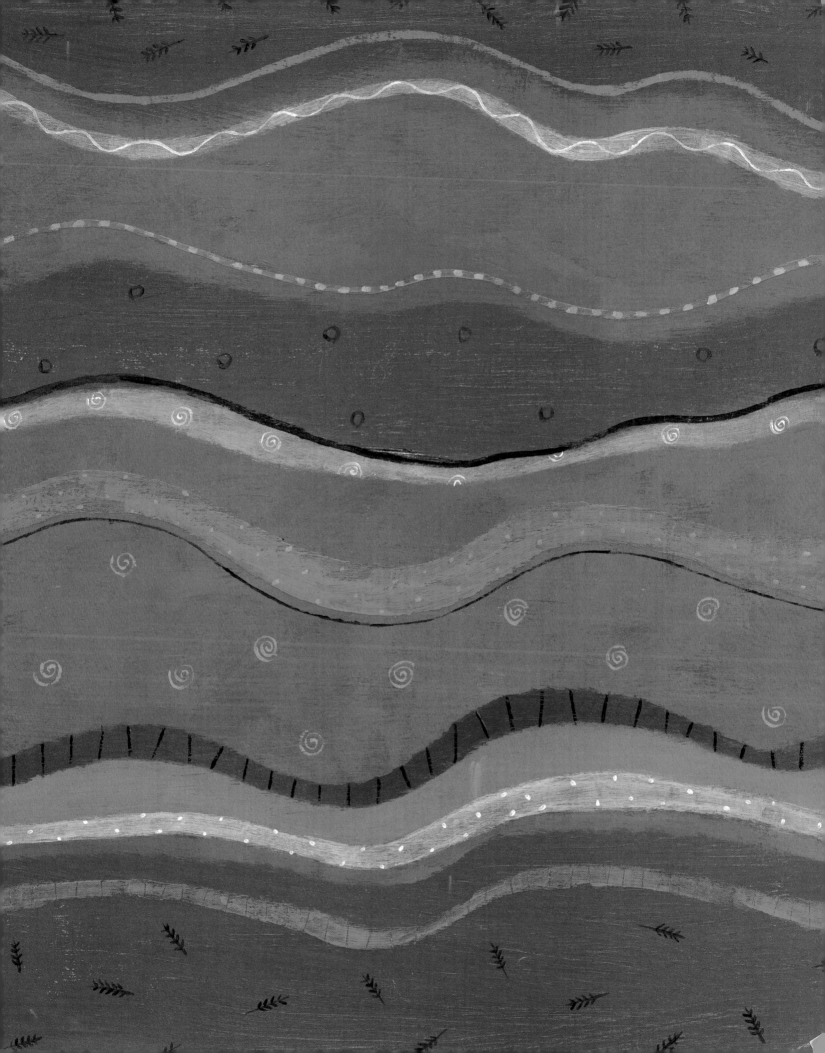

This edition published in the UK in 2006 and in the USA in 2007 by
Frances Lincoln Children's Books,
74-77 White Lion Street, London N1 9PF
www.franceslincoln.com

First published in Great Britain in 1999 by Doubleday Childrens,
an imprint of Random House Children's Publishers UK

First published in the USA in 1999 by Orchard Books, an imprint of Scholastic

British Library Cataloguing in Publication Data
available on request

ISBN 13: 978-1-84507-700-6

Printed in China

5 7 9 8 6

www.anholt.co.uk

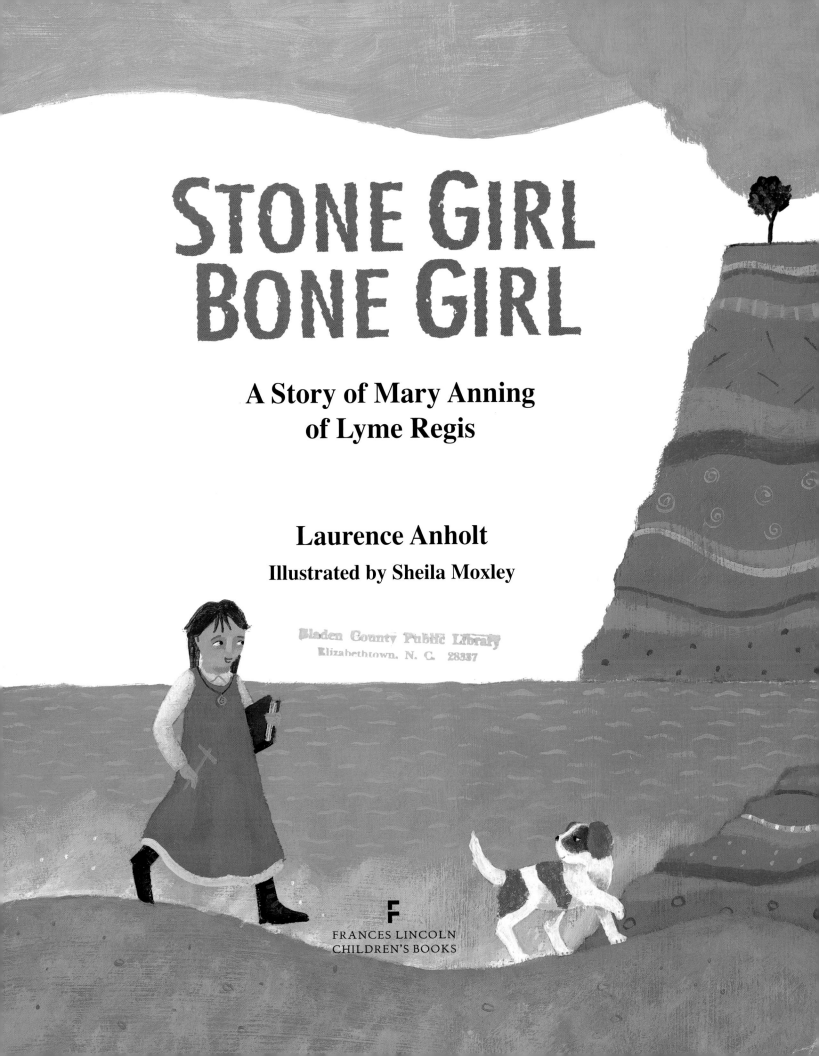

STONE GIRL
BONE GIRL

A Story of Mary Anning
of Lyme Regis

Laurence Anholt

Illustrated by Sheila Moxley

F
FRANCES LINCOLN
CHILDREN'S BOOKS

When Mary Anning was a baby she was struck by lightning. It split a huge elm tree and threw Mary right out of her nurse's arms.

Her father was in his carpenter's shop when he heard the terrible news. He dropped his hammer and ran through the stormy streets of Lyme Regis. Gently, he lifted the limp body of his little daughter and his tears flowed like rain.

But then, an extraordinary thing happened... Mary Anning slowly opened her eyes. She reached out a tiny hand and touched the amazed face of her father. And the little girl began to smile.

It was then her father realised - Mary Anning was no ordinary girl.

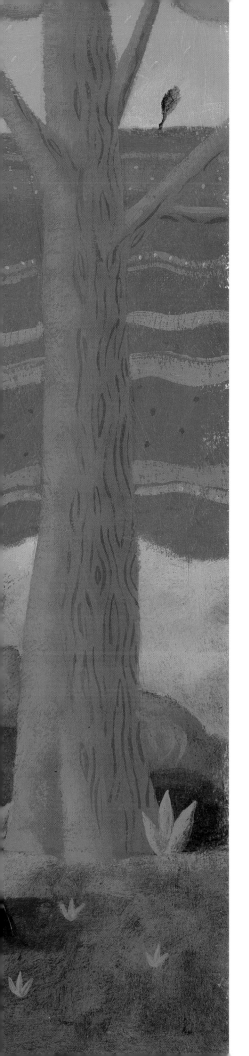

The years rolled by like waves. Mary grew into a clever girl. "A mind as quick as lightning!" her mother teased.

Mary had few friends, except her father, whom she adored. Like everyone else in the town, she called him "Pepper" because of his speckled beard.

One Saturday, Pepper closed his workshop early. He took Mary down to the cliffs by the crashing sea. She held tightly to his hand because she knew how dangerous it could be. The clay cliffs at Lyme Regis are soft as melting chocolate. Mary had sometimes seen huge slabs of land slipping and tumbling to the beach below.

Pepper had stories of whole fields on the cliff tops which had disappeared beneath the feet of grazing cattle. He knew a place, he said, where half a farmhouse sat balanced on the cliff edge. He and his quarrymen friend had peered over and seen the remains of the kitchen and even the garden gate, smashed to splinters on the rocks below.

When they came to the place called Black Ven, Pepper reached into his pocket and, to Mary's surprise, took out his best steel hammer. He knelt beside a large rock of dried clay and began carefully tapping away.

"What are you looking for?" asked Mary, dancing about on the sand.

"Just be patient," laughed Pepper.

He worked as carefully as if he were making a fine piece of furniture. Mary bent closer. There was something hidden there! Right inside the rock!

At last Pepper pulled it free and handed the thing to Mary.

"It... it's TREASURE!" she gasped.

"It's what we call a little Snakestone," smiled Pepper. "Just a Curiosity. A present for you, Mary girl."

It was the most beautiful thing Mary had ever seen. Back in the workshop, Pepper polished the Snakestone and hung it on a string for Mary - like a perfect necklace.

That night Mary couldn't sleep. Her head swirled with thoughts like the twisting golden stone. "The cliffs are full of treasure," she whispered over and over again.

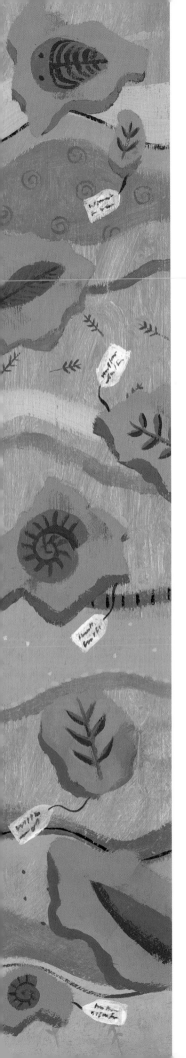

From that day on, Mary spent every spare moment searching for the Curiosities. She had sharp eyes and found them everywhere, in every shape and size - tiny shiny ones, marble ones as big as millstones, others straight as stone fingers, or delicate like plants.

Pepper taught her their strange, magical names - "Thunderbolts, Fairy's Hearts, Crocodile's Teeth, Devil's Toenails". He let Mary have her own special drawer in the workshop for her collection.

But the other children laughed and teased when they saw Mary hunting near the cliffs. Someone made up a rhyme - "Stone Girl, Bone Girl. Out on your own Girl!" - until Mary ran crying to Pepper.

That winter was the wettest and stormiest the town had known. Great waves smashed the little houses and the cliffs became softer and more dangerous still. So Mary stayed away.

The cold, damp air made Pepper feel ill. He looked old and tired and sometimes he coughed so loudly that Mary felt afraid.

O ne evening some rich ladies came to Pepper's workshop. Mary knew who they were - the Philpot sisters who lived together in a fine house high above the town. Scientists, people said.

The youngest of the ladies, Annie Philpot, wanted Pepper to build a glass-fronted cabinet. "To display Curiosities," she said.

Mary jumped up. She couldn't believe that someone else was interested in Curiosities.

"Excuse me," Mary said nervously, "would you like to see my collection?" And she pulled open the drawer.

"Oh!" gasped the ladies. "What wonderful fossils!"

Fossils? Mary had never heard the word. The Misses Philpot smiled. They could see that Mary didn't know much about her collection.

"I'll tell you what, Mary," said Annie Philpot, "when Pepper has finished my little cabinet, why don't you bring it to us? We could have some tea and then we will show you our collection."

For three long weeks she waited for Pepper to finish the cabinet, but he seemed to be working more slowly than ever. Mary was very worried about him.

But at last the elm cabinet was finished. The wood was from the very same tree that had been struck by lightning and had almost killed baby Mary. She thought it was the most handsome thing that Pepper had ever made.

Slowly, Pepper wrapped the cabinet in brown paper and tied it with string. His old hands were shaking as he kissed Mary.

Mary had never seen anything like the Philpots' house. There were expensive rugs in every room and maids to serve the tea. Most wonderful of all was the collection of Curiosities. The Misses Philpot explained that the fossils were the remains of ancient sea creatures that had been preserved in the clay.

Everything was so interesting that Mary forgot to be nervous. Then Annie Philpot showed her a huge tooth she had found.

"From a great sea monster," she said. She told Mary she believed the rest of the creature was still out there, hidden in the cliffs. "If anyone could ever find that, Mary! That would be the greatest treasure of all."

It was nearly dark when Mary ran down the hill. As soon as she pushed open the workshop door, she knew that something was wrong.

The workshop was so quiet after Pepper died. To Mary it felt as if half her world had fallen away, like the farmhouse on the cliff edge. And there was no money. Her mother began to sell everything she could think of, and still they went to bed hungry.

One evening, Mary wandered up to the churchyard. A heavy fog hung over everything. Ragged clouds dragged at a lemon-slice moon. As she came to the stone that marked Pepper's grave, something moved in the darkness.

For a moment Mary was afraid, but coming closer she realised it was nothing but a funny little dog...a little dog with a coat like speckled pepper!

The dog bounded over and licked Mary's face. When she turned to walk home, the little dog came too. At last it ran into the workshop and curled under the table.

"Perhaps you need a friend too," laughed Mary. From that moment, Mary and the dog were never apart.

That summer the town was full of holiday-makers. As Mary and her dog watched the rich ladies and gentlemen wandering the streets, she suddenly had an idea - perhaps she could sell her Curiosities!

She dragged a table from the workshop onto the pavement and carefully arranged the fossils from her collection - all except the Snakestone around her neck. That she would never part with. She wrote a small sign in her best handwriting, "CURIOSITIES FOR SALE". Then Mary Anning and the little dog sat down to wait.

The first to pass were a group of children. They began laughing and pointing at poor Mary. "Stone Girl, Bone Girl! Out on your own Girl!" they shouted.

All day Mary waited. She was just about to pack away her table when a group of ladies and gentlemen came by.

"How fascinating!" said a lady.

"What are they?" asked someone else.

"This one would make a delightful brooch..."

"Or a garden ornament..."

And so Mary Anning sold her first fossils - and as the rich people strolled away, Mary felt the weight of coins in her pocket.

"I knew I was right!" she whispered to her dog. "These aren't just ordinary stones - they really are treasures. If only I could find that sea monster!"

All summer, Mary searched for Curiosities for her shop. She borrowed books about fossils from the Misses Philpot and learnt everything she could.

Her mother was delighted with the money that Mary was earning, but she was worried about Mary alone on the dangerous cliffs. Mary reassured her that the little dog would run for help in an emergency.

As she searched, Mary thought more and more about the giant sea monster and about the cliffs in prehistoric times. She imagined fantastic landscapes inhabited by extraordinary creatures.

One morning, Mary was so busy day dreaming, she didn't notice that her dog had wandered away. She ran along the beach, calling for him, but he was nowhere to be seen.

At last, she heard a faint barking and, looking up, she saw the speckled dog high on the sloping side of the cliff.

Mary called for him to come down, but the little dog wouldn't move. He was furiously scratching at something in the clay.

Mary had no choice. She began slowly to climb the rock face. At last she reached the little ledge where the dog was standing. Her heart missed a beat. She couldn't believe what she saw... Grinning up at Mary was an enormous skull! The little dog had found the sea monster.

All morning, Mary scraped furiously with Pepper's hammer. There was more than a skull - a whole skeleton, perhaps. But it was far too big for Mary to cope with on her own. Who could help her? Suddenly, she remembered Pepper's old friends, the quarrymen.

Leaving the little dog to guard the monster, Mary Anning climbed carefully down to the beach, then ran as fast as she could to the quarry.

"I've found it!" she shouted. "I've found the sea monster!"

In less than ten minutes, Mary was leading a group of quarrymen carrying picks and shovels up the side of the cliff.